Younguncle
Comes to Town

by **VANDANA SINGH**

illustrated by **B. M. KAMATH**

VIKING

J Sing

In loving memory of my grandparents,
Ranchor and Sharda Prasad, who taught me
by example the meaning of the Sanskrit Great Saying:
"Tat Tvam Asi."

VIKING
Published by Penguin Group
Penguin Young Readers Group, 345 Hudson Street,
New York, New York 10014, U.S.A.

Penguin Books Ltd, Registered Offices: 80 Strand, London WC2R 0RL, England

First published in the United States in 2006 by Viking, a division of Penguin Young Readers Group

1 3 5 7 9 10 8 6 4 2

Text copyright © Vandana Singh, 2004
Interior illustrations copyright © B. M. Kamath, 2004
Jacket illustration copyright © Sandy Nichols, 2006
All rights reserved.
First published in 2004 in India by Young Zubaan.

LIBRARY OF CONGRESS CATALOGING-IN-PUBLICATION DATA
Singh, Vandana.
Younguncle comes to town / by Vandana Singh ; interior illustrations by B.M. Kamath.
p. cm.
Summary: In a small town in northern India, three siblings await their father's youngest brother,
Younguncle, who is said to be somewhat eccentric.
ISBN 0-670-06051-8 (hardcover)
[1. Uncles—Fiction. 2. Eccentrics and eccentricities—Fiction. 3. India—Fiction.]
I. Kamath, B. M., ill. II. Title.
PZ7.S61754You 2006
[Fic]—dc22
2005014146

Printed in U.S.A.
Set in Life
Book design by Kelley McIntyre

Contents

Younguncle
Comes to Town

One rainy afternoon, three children sat looking out of an open window, their fingers curled around the metal grillwork. The rain had come down like a great moving curtain, making the narrow lanes sparkle, turning the roadside ditches into torrential streams. They had watched a procession of cows canter off toward the shelter of the enormous neem tree around the corner; they had seen neighbors hurry past under wet, black umbrellas; they had seen cars and rickshaws and an oxcart splash

1

their way through the waterlogged street. Now the rain had slowed to a murmur and the lane was empty except for a water buffalo, its black hide agleam, standing meditatively under the shisham tree on the other side.

"When will he get here?" nine-year-old Sarita asked for the fiftieth time. Her brother, Ravi, who was two years younger, said: "He'll get here; let's just wait a little while longer. I like watching the road when it rains."

"Oohwah!" agreed the baby, who stood between them on the broad windowsill.

Their father had told them that his youngest brother, universally known as Younguncle, was coming to live with them. He was supposed to arrive today. Nobody had gone to the railway station to pick him up, because Younguncle had not told them what time he would be arriving.

"That is just like him," the children's father had said with a sigh. "He likes to do things his own way. Why, he has just spent the last two years wandering all over the country, having all kinds of hair-raising adventures. He's a good fellow, but he needs to settle down. That is why your mother and I have invited him to come and live with us."

"What is his real name?" Sarita had asked then.

"Nobody remembers. He has always been

called Younguncle. He says he prefers it that way—although it is quite ridiculous to be called Younguncle even by one's parents. But he has always been a little different from other people."

All this sounded quite exciting to the children. They had been waiting since lunch for Younguncle's arrival. During the afternoon there had been a procession of people at the house: the barber, the oil massage man, the mango seller, and a neighbor or two. The milkman, Ramu, had come and gone with his cow, Janaki. But there was still no sign of Younguncle.

"Do you remember what he looks like?" Ravi asked Sarita. The last time Younguncle had visited had been some years ago, before he had gone off to college.

"Not really," Sarita said. "I remember he was long and thin and liked to make noises like

4

a monkey. But I was very small then, and you were just a baby."

"Gah!" said the baby disbelievingly. She couldn't imagine either of her siblings as babies. The possibility that a universe had existed before her birth seemed positively absurd to her.

Just as she was contemplating her latest biological classification scheme (based on the number of legs a creature had, so that cars and cows belonged to one family, and humans, birds, and bicycles to another), she noticed something. She sat up in excitement, pointing with a plump finger. A curious figure was making its way down the street.

He was a long, lanky young man wearing a battered tin plate on his head as though it were a crown. The rain drummed musically on the plate, making it tip about and sparkle on his head, and from time to time he would reach up and adjust the brim. He had an amiable smile on his face, and was looking about him with eyes full of approval, as though the rainstorm had been just the thing he had ordered with his lunch. In one hand he held a cup of tea, one of those earthen cups you still find in small-town railway stations in North India. He would sip from the cup, then hold it out into the rain, and sip again. With his other hand he was helping a rickshaw man wheel a rickshaw piled with bags and wooden cases covered with soggy news-paper. He was conversing animatedly with the rickshaw man, who was smiling broadly and gesticulating. The two men were both soaking wet, although neither of them seemed to notice.

They came to a stop in front of the house. At once, the young man noticed the water buffalo under the shisham tree on the other side of the lane, and greeted it solemnly. The water buffalo allowed him to scratch its head and mooed conversationally, upon which the young man said something in reply, gave the animal a respectful pat, and crossed the road to the gate of the house. He opened the gate with a flourish, ushered in the rickshaw man, and walked with him up the short driveway toward the house. They came to a stop at the steps that led up to the front door.

"What do you think, my friend, is this a good place for them?" said the young man, looking around him at the lush, rain-soaked garden and the dripping trees.

"I think so, sir. Look at all those trees! It's a much better place for them than the railway station."

At this point the young man suddenly became aware of the watching children. A big grin of delight nearly split his face in half. He

waved madly, set his teacup down on the driveway, and leapt onto the rickshaw. He tore the
newspaper wrapping off two large cases that,
the children now saw, were small, crude cages
made of wire and wood that seemed to be filled
with fluttering movement. He fiddled with the
cage doors and suddenly there was a great flurry
of wings and color, and a host of birds flew out:
green and yellow parakeets, tiny multicolored
munias, doves and pigeons with iridescent wings.
They flew in all directions and vanished.

The baby laughed and clapped her hands.
The children looked at each other and smiled,
and then, lifting the baby off the sill, they all ran
downstairs.

Downstairs, Younguncle was explaining the
loss of his umbrella and brandishing the tin
plate, which had three holes in it. "It was a fair
exchange with the boy from whom I bought

these birds—a mere umbrella for this antique plate with which three generations of bird-sellers have fed their stock and fended off the rain. . . ." The children's mother was talking at the same time about how he would catch his Death of Cold if he didn't go to his room At Once and Dry Off. The rickshaw man was helping to bring the suitcases into the house, discussing the state of the monsoons with the children's father, and they could already smell the pakoras frying in the kitchen and the aroma of fresh mint chutney. On the dining table there was tea steaming in the pot and an array of milk sweets cut into diamonds, silvered as though by the rain.

Younguncle greeted the children with the big smile that seemed to belong so naturally to his face, and drew them to him. Unmindful of his wet clothes, he sat down on the floor, so that the children would be eye-to-eye with him, and began to unpack the largest suitcase right there in the middle of the drawing room. It was filled to the brim with the most unusual things: an enormous conch shell he had found on the shores of the Arabian Sea, a fragile piece of coral that had washed up on a beach in the Andaman Islands, a sculpture of twisted vines that had been given to him by an artistically in-clined monkey from the forests of Assam. . . .

"This is all very well," the children's father said, admiring a beautiful stone pot that Young-uncle had obtained from a village in central India. "But really, Younguncle, it is high time you settled down now."

Younguncle winked at the children.

"You will find nobody more settled down than I, Elder Brother," he said. "I shall put down roots like the proverbial banyan tree and become duller than an elderly accountant. And the children will keep me in order. Right, children?"

Ravi and Sarita smiled shyly at their uncle. The baby, however, subjected him to her trademark penetrating stare, in order to gauge how serious he was, and to search his soul for blemishes. In fact, she was also filing him away mentally as "family," "two-legged" (like bird and bicycle), and "possible steed."

"Oohwah!" said the baby approvingly.

Younguncle
and the Pickpockets

Younguncle settled in very quickly, and soon it seemed to the children that he had always lived with them. He told them all kinds of stories—funny ones and scary ones, quiet ones and adventurous ones; he played noisy games of *kho-kho* with them, read to the baby from books ranging from philosophy to physics, and helped the older children with their homework. Within a month, he had gotten to know everyone in the neighborhood, and wherever he went, people would stop to talk to him about a nephew's wedding, or their arthritis, or the latest cricket scores.

Within four months he had been through three jobs, a fact that worried the children's father and led to much discussion amongst concerned neighbors. The trouble with Young-uncle, people said, was not that he couldn't hold down a job, but that he took his jobs too seriously. Well, maybe serious is not the word, people would say. Enthusiastic. That was what he was. To the point that sane people—that is, people who were boring and conventional—got quite uncomfortable with him around. After a while, his employers would become cold toward him and he would take the hint and leave.

He first worked at a car repair place. He was supposed to be the junior manager there, but he got so interested in the way the cars were put on platforms and raised into the air to have their insides fixed that he came home every day covered with black grease. He also acquired the habit of imitating the sounds of cars with various afflictions—cars with gear problems, cars with choked exhausts, and so on. He got so good at his job that, simply by the sound the car made, he could tell precisely what was wrong with it.

The children really enjoyed the time that Younguncle was a car mechanic, because he got serious about cars and traffic. On his daily walks with them to the big park on the other side of the neighborhood, he would point out the kinds of cars that passed by, the possible problems the cars might have, and the possible temperaments of the owners. Younguncle trained them to begin walking in step in slow motion as soon as they came near a speed bump. There were only a few traffic signs in the little town where they lived, and most of them were painted on the road so that they could not be stolen. If the sign said "Stop," Younguncle would stop with a realistic belching and grinding and squealing of brakes, and smile kindly at the people who were staring at him and the children. He could toot like the horn of a police car, and wail like an ambulance siren as well. When he saw somebody disobeying traffic rules, which was very often, he would make these sounds and startle the errant motorist. The driver and his passengers would look around guiltily. Since most people in the area knew Younguncle, and since Younguncle looked particularly innocent holding the baby, the drivers would wave and smile at them while looking around nervously for the source of the sound. Most of the time the drivers would begin to behave after that, not because they were afraid of being fined, but because they did not want to have to buy the traffic policeman sweets from the Corner Sweet Shop, which was what usually happened if you were caught.

Not long after that, Younguncle got a job in a big tailoring shop. Again, he was supposed to be a junior manager there, but he found the work too interesting. He learned to cut and sew, and to use a sewing machine. At home, his sister-in-law, the children's mother, began to give him little sewing chores, such as mending a tear in her husband's shirt or her son's trousers. Younguncle also managed to repair three of his own shirts that had had holes bitten in them by the baby. It was the baby's aim in life to eat an entire shirt of Younguncle's, and Younguncle was forever thwarting the baby's schemes.

But what the children liked best about this job of Younguncle's was that Younguncle learned to imitate a sewing machine. He was always ready to make the sound for them—the hum, the *taca-taca-taca*, the whine of the thread unspooling. And one night this talent came in very useful.

One of the ladies who worked at the tailor's shop was feeling unwell. She had been very slow at her work that day and was afraid that if she didn't finish it, the boss would be angry. The customer was expecting it the very next day. So Younguncle whispered to her that he would finish the job after working hours. When the other employees had gone home, the boss told Younguncle to lock up, and left. Younguncle shut the door and began to work.

Darkness fell. Younguncle was working with a small flashlight on because he did not want the light to shine through the windows. The boss might ride by in his car and notice. The evening wore on and long shadows fell across the room. At long last, the job was done. Younguncle took the suit he had finished and hung it on the rack with the completed pieces.

Just as he did so, he heard a noise. Quickly he turned off the flashlight and stood in the darkness, his heart thumping. He heard a soft, scraping sound, and a tentative footstep. There was somebody in the shop!

There was a completed dress hanging on the rack near Younguncle—a big, white monstrosity of a thing, meant for a very large young woman who was going to wear it in a play. Immediately, Younguncle crept under the gargantuan folds of the dress. The thief came closer and began feeling around the clothes.

Younguncle pushed his head up through the collar of the dress and saw that the thief was now trying to open the locked strongbox. What to do?

The sewing machines stood about the floor of the shop, draped in their covers. The long racks of finished clothes and the shadow of the grinning mannequin standing silently in the display window made the place look ghostly.

Then Younguncle had an idea. He began

doing his imitation of a sewing machine at full throttle. The thief jumped, startled, and looked around at the room full of stillness and shadows. Where was the sound coming from? Were there really eyes peering at him over the top of that hideous monster of a dress? He yelped and fled. Younguncle was briefly a hero after that event.

A short while later, a big, fancy stationery store opened in the marketplace. It was too big and too fancy for such a small town, so people would come just to see all the things that were on display—the fine brushes and paints, the different kinds of paper. Nobody bought any of the fancy stuff. Having recently lost his job at the tailoring shop, Younguncle applied for a job at the stationer's.

The stationer was from a big city and had big-city notions.

"What's your name?" he asked, writing busily on a piece of paper.

"Younguncle," said Younguncle.

"What? Don't be foolish. I cannot call you uncle. What is your real name?"

"Don't know. I've forgotten. Everyone calls me Younguncle."

The man frowned.

"I'm giving you the job," he said, "but we have to give you a proper name. We are a big chain store, not one of these provincial little shops. Let me see. . . . I think we'll call you Hemant."

Younguncle had to wear a label on his shirt that said "Hemant," but he always introduced himself as Younguncle. People who knew him would say: "Why are you wearing Hemant's shirt, Younguncle?"

"Because Hemant doesn't want to wear it."

Younguncle got so enthusiastic about the art supplies in the store that people started buying them. He got permission from his boss to demonstrate how the different kinds of papers and pens were to be used. He would make little drawings for his younger customers that enchanted them so much that they would end up buying the materials.

"Draw me a man and a horse," a child would say. Younguncle would draw a picture of a horse riding a man, and the child would go home with a sheaf of art paper and drawing pens, all happy and excited, with Younguncle's drawing carefully folded under his arm. He drew a princess holding the reins of a pony that was flying up in the air; he drew a large cat and a dog taking some children for a walk. Sometimes he would take the pictures home for his nephew and nieces, although he would have to keep the drawings out of reach of the baby. The baby had recently become capable of crawling and was on a mission to taste, chew, and spit up everything in the universe. Younguncle had a few philosophical discussions with the baby about this, pointing out that there were better ways to know the essence of a thing than by devouring and re-gurgitating it, but the baby remained unconvinced.

Then Younguncle got what the children always considered his dream job: deputy-stationmaster-in-training at the railway station.

"What is a whatever-that-was-in-training?" Sarita asked him.

"A person who trains trains," said Younguncle soberly. After that, the children always imagined Younguncle telling the trains where to go and when to go, and sending them, with a wave of the hand, to far-off places like Varanasi and Delhi.

The train station was a noisy, untidy place filled with people in a hurry, people waiting, people asleep on baggage, beggars and pickpockets, and, of course, the porters in their tattered red-and-white uniforms, helping people carry their luggage to and from the trains. Younguncle loved it. Soon he could screech like a train's whistle, and go "chook-chook" better than anyone.

He taught the children that old Hindi song that goes "Rail gaari! Rail gaari! *Chook-chook, chook-chook!*" which means "Train! Train! *Chook-chook, chook-chook!*" It is a funny song, full of all the noises the train makes and the lilt and rhythm of its motion.

One day, the children and their mother came to visit Younguncle at the railway station. They fought their way through the crowds to the stationmaster's office. Younguncle was very pleased to see them.

Just then, the stationmaster told Younguncle that the train from Kolkata, which had been running late, had now arrived. The announcer was having a tea break, so Younguncle was supposed to announce the arrival of the train over the loudspeaker.

Younguncle was thrilled. Instead of saying "May I have your Attention Please?" he began his announcement by making a very loud train-whistle sound that made the pigeons fly off the roofs in shock. Then, to the delight of the children, Younguncle began to sing: "Rail gaari!

Rail gaari! The Howrah Express—*chook-chook, chook-chook!*—is here! Rail gaari!"

The harried, stressed people milling about on the platform began to smile. Only the station-master didn't smile. He was a bad-tempered man who liked to drink endless cups of tea and have a man come in and massage his head with coconut oil. He made everyone else do his work and lectured them about professionalism. Later, after the relatives had left, he scolded Younguncle.

Younguncle listened with great attention, as though what the master was saying was of international significance. All the while he kept wiping his left ear down with his hand.

Finally the master could not take it.

"Why on earth are you doing that?" he barked.

"Because all your words are running into my

26

right ear and out of the left ear, and I am trying to keep them from tangling in my hair," said Younguncle blandly.

One of Younguncle's most interesting adventures occurred during his stint as a deputy-stationmaster-in-training. One day, the stationmaster came up to him and told him: "The merchant Paytu Lal has made a very strong complaint about pickpockets in the railway station harassing his employees. He lost a purse of a thousand rupees yesterday! He wants the criminals caught. The police have been useless, so I want you to do something about it."

Now, Paytu Lal was the richest merchant in town. He owned not only all the expensive shops such as the jewelry store and the Silk Sari Palace, but a string of little ones, too, selling liquor and cigarettes near the poor part of the town, and cheap magazines and cosmetics made of toxic substances through small, ramshackle neighborhood stores. He had a stomach like a very large pumpkin and a large, bristling mustache. His seven sons did all the dirty work, running the stores and cheating the customers. His five grandsons rode loud motorbikes all over town, startling and harassing pedestrians and motorists. The police did nothing because Paytu Lal was too powerful for them. The politicians went to him for campaign funds. He had dirty fingers.

Nobody said "Paytu Lal is a thief," for the same reason that nobody says "The sun will rise in the east tomorrow."

So when Younguncle heard that Paytu Lal's people were being robbed at the railway station, his first reaction was "Let us give the pickpockets a medal!" But then he had to deal with the pickpockets' other victims. Like the lady who had stepped off the train to buy mangoes and had her purse stolen, with her ticket inside it. Or the old man who had come to town for his granddaughter's wedding, to find that all his money was gone. Younguncle gave all this some thought.

Finally he went to his friend Kanhaiya. Kanhaiya ran a small and very successful tea shack near Younguncle's own neighborhood. Kanhaiya had been a pickpocket once, and a very successful one. Then one night the goddess Lakshmi had come to him in a dream, holding a teapot. Kanhaiya had taken this as an omen that wealth would come more easily to him via the honest trade of a tea seller, and since then he had focused his considerable talents on the brewing of the perfect cup of masala chai.

When he heard what Younguncle had to say,

however, Kanhaiya shook his head.

"I don't want anything to do with that life anymore, my friend, even if it is to apprehend the pickpockets."

"But I don't want you to apprehend the pickpockets," Younguncle said. He leaned closer and began to whisper. "This is what I want you to do. . . ."

So Kanhaiya put the tea shack in the hands of his son and came with Younguncle to the railway station. Kanhaiya looked around appreciatively.

"This brings back memories," he said, sighing. Then he pointed. "See that fellow over there, loitering, looking at the bulletin board? He's one of them. I can spot them very easily, you know. I had the sharpest eyes and the quickest fingers in the business."

Kanhaiya got to work.

The pickpockets soon found that something rather strange was happening to them. One of them had just slipped away after robbing an old widow who had come to town to live with her son, bringing all of her savings with her. But when the thief got outside the station, he found that his pockets were mysteriously empty. Meanwhile, back on the platform, the old woman was wailing and cursing and sobbing into her sari.

"It's my stupid neighbor and her new-fangled ideas! I always keep the money down my blouse, like a sensible person, but she had to give me a purse as a farewell gift!"

A crowd collected around her, clicking their tongues in sympathy. Then Kanhaiya came up to her holding her purse.

"You dropped this, Auntie?"

The old woman looked at him suspiciously,

opened the purse, and began checking the contents. Then she smiled.

"Thank you, my son! May you be blessed a hundred times with good fortune!"

She gave him a ten-rupee note, but Kanhaiya's true reward (or so he said) was the look of rapturous gratitude on her face.

So the pickpockets found that whenever they robbed from ordinary people, their pockets were picked in turn. Whoever did it was incredibly quick and practically invisible. It scared them.

But when they robbed Paytu Lal and his cohorts, nothing happened. Nobody interfered with them, and they came home with riches.

Finally they got the hint and began to concentrate only on the merchant and his people. Paytu Lal continued to make threats and shout orders over the phone to the stationmaster, but nothing came of it. Nothing at all.

The only time that the pickpockets were robbed of wealth they had lifted from Paytu Lal was when a new wing was being built at the local public hospital. The hospital got a rather substantial anonymous donation.

Younguncle enjoyed his job so much that he worked at the railway station for over a year. The family was pleased—they thought he was finally beginning to settle down. Since it was a government job, the stationmaster could not fire him without a lot of trouble. But one day Younguncle left of his own accord. When pressed, he shrugged off the questions and gave no reply but an enigmatic smile.

So Younguncle went from job to job. He learned many things and made innumerable friends. His elder brother was often worried about Younguncle's future. What was the use of a college bachelor's degree if it didn't get you a nice, steady job? All this flitting about from job to job was wasteful. But his wife, Younguncle's sister-in-law, reassured him.

"He's still Young," she said. She had a way of speaking in words that began with Capital Letters. "He is gaining Experience. At some point people will recognize his Worth. He will also Mature. Maybe we should look for a Wife for him—after all, your parents already have Someone in Mind for your sister, Rekha. It's Hard for them to look for Someone for Younguncle, since they live in another town. Besides, I would like Younguncle and his wife to live with us. He is so Good with the Children!"

Her husband nodded.

It is a good thing Younguncle did not hear this conversation, because he had a terrible fear of being managed. His sister-in-law was a good manager—she ran the household, the children, and her husband, and let Young-uncle go his own way, mostly. But a wife! A wife would take the reins of his soul and hold them in her soft, henna-colored little hands and say, *"Chal merey ghorey tik tik tik!"* which is Hindi for *"Giddy-up!"* Younguncle was not ready for that yet.

So how did Younguncle foil the well-meaning schemes of his brother and sister-in-law to get him married off? Ah, that is a story still not told.

Younguncle
Saves His Sister
from a Terrible Fate

S ometimes Younguncle would leave town for short trips. The children always hated his going because the house seemed so strange and quiet without him, but always he promised to come back soon. "Every trip I take becomes a story," he would tell them, "a new story for you when I return." The children imagined that with every step of his journey, a word or a syllable of the story was written—and that without the trip, somehow, the story would have to remain incomplete, or even worse, go wrong. When Younguncle returned from his first trip they realized how true this was.

He was in between two of his many jobs, so he decided to visit his old hometown to see his parents and youngest sister. All the relatives and friends were very excited. Younguncle's parents had found a match for his sister, their only unmarried child other than Younguncle himself. The Boy, as everyone called him, was highly eligible; he was from a well-to-do family that had moved into town very recently. How recently? Oh, about ten years ago. Younguncle's sister Rekha had liked the Boy, Praveen, best out of the seventeen that her parents had arranged for her to see. He had charm. He had class. He was from a big city, and knew so much more about the world than the provincial people of the town. His clothes were all elegant and fashionable. Rekha and Praveen were allowed to meet at family functions and to go see an occasional movie (under the strict but kindly eye of a relative), and she was very much in love with him.

But on his second day home, Younguncle found Rekha crying alone in her room.

"What's the matter?"

"Oh, Younguncle, I don't think I want to marry Praveen!"

"But you are in love with him!"

Rekha wiped her eyes.

"Yes, well I thought I was. But lately he has been showing me his true colors. He is a mean-minded man, Younguncle! He makes little digs at me when Ma and Baba aren't nearby. He *says* things!"

She suppressed a little sob.

"I think that whole family is mean. The

washerwoman was telling me they pay their servants a pittance! They still owe her fifty-seven rupees!

"Praveen thinks my favorite blue sari looks ugly! He thinks my hair is not long enough! He thinks I should not continue with college! 'Anything beyond a bachelor's degree is not respectable for a woman,' he says!"

Her wide, tragic eyes filled with tears again.

"You know what the worst thing is? He's a bore! Talking to him is like talking to my old school principal! I tried to tell him a joke yesterday, you know, that silly one about the snake charmer's mother-in-law and the camel, and he didn't even laugh! He said virtuous women don't crack jokes!"

"This is serious," Younguncle said. "Have you told Ma and Baba?"

Rekha began to sob in earnest.

"They think I am making a big fuss over nothing. They think I am just nervous because everyone gets nervous before marriage. All the relatives and friends have been told the wedding will be in September, and it will be a big disgrace if they cancel everything—people will say our family does not keep its word!"

She looked up at Younguncle, her face red and splotched with tears.

"The only way I can get out of this is to run away or . . . or . . . or die!"

"That is not practical," Younguncle said severely. "We are not in some silly Bollywood movie. We need brains, not melodrama."

Younguncle became very thoughtful.

"Leave it to me," was all he would say to Rekha.

The next day the Boy and his parents came for tea. Younguncle's parents introduced Younguncle as their youngest son. Rekha's prospec-tive mother-in-law grilled him on his job, his work habits, his prospects. Then the phone rang. It was a call from Younguncle's married older sister in America. His parents excused them-selves and left the room to take the call.

At once, Younguncle began bouncing up and down on the sofa, making soft hooting noises. He leapt across the coffee table and pulled Praveen's hair, then slapped him gently on both cheeks. He rolled his eyes and danced around the room, giggling. The three guests got up in alarm and anger. They glared at Rekha, who had gotten over her initial shock (she was quick on the uptake) and was sitting demurely at her place.

"What is he doing? Is he having some sort of fit?" said Praveen's mother.

"Some more tea?" Younguncle said politely,

picking up the lady's cup as though nothing had happened. His parents came back into the room, apologizing and smiling. They sensed that something was wrong.

"Please, please, sit down. Surely you won't go just yet? What . . . what is the matter?"

Smiling distractedly, and giving Younguncle rather dubious looks, the guests sat down again. They fidgeted and kept glancing at Younguncle throughout the conversation. For the rest of the afternoon, Younguncle was the model of the good host.

Later, after they had left, Younguncle found out that the Boy and his family lived two streets away in a big two-story brick house.

The next morning Praveen was woken up by a sound from the window.

Splat!

A large, soft object came whizzing through

the air and burst against the window glass.

Praveen's family had air conditioners in every room (a fact that they did not keep hidden from those less fortunate than themselves), so the windows were all kept closed. Praveen got out of bed, half fearful, half indignant. He looked cautiously out of the window.

That fiend, his betrothed's younger brother, was perched in the branches of the big mango tree, pelting the window with rotten fruit!

Seeing him, Younguncle began to sway on the branches and hoot. He waved and smiled. He threw another volley of mangoes.

Praveen gripped the edge of the windowsill. Hot anger coursed through him. He rushed off to wake the household.

As he went down the stairs, the doorbell rang. By the time he got to the dining room, Younguncle was sitting at the table, politely accepting

43

tea and samosas. He waved at Praveen.

"I was in the neighborhood, and I thought I would drop in."

Praveen's parents were forced to put up with Younguncle for an hour. He was courteous, charming, and utterly normal. Meanwhile Praveen scowled at him and fidgeted. At long last, Younguncle rose to leave.

"It has been so nice to see you again. I look forward to the time when you will all be part of my family," Younguncle said. Suddenly his air of normality vanished. He took the last samosa, crumbled it in his hands, sprinkled it on Praveen's head, jumped up and down three times, and ran out of the house, giggling.

Two days later there was a big party at Praveen's house. His brother and sister-in-law had just returned from a trip to Europe, and the family was anxious to show off the trinkets they had purchased on the trip. Rekha and her parents were invited, of course, but the note from Praveen's parents asked them please not to bring Younguncle.

"Not bring Younguncle? What are they trying to do, insult us?" rumbled Younguncle's father. He looked at his wife. "Last time they were here, Praveen's father drew me aside and began to ask me if Younguncle had a mental problem. Mental problem! I'll give him a mental problem!"

"Do calm down," his wife said, holding the note and frowning. "My own feeling is that there is some misunderstanding. Someone must be spreading rumors. I am sure once we talk to them it will all be cleared up."

"We'll take Younguncle," said her husband, still fuming. "Let us see what they do!"

Praveen's house was full of people. There

were ladies in silk saris chattering away. There were children running around. The TV was on in several rooms. A cheap metal Eiffel Tower was being admired by a knot of guests.

"Ah, Paris! Or rather *Pah-reee*, as they say," Praveen's brother was saying. He was a big, important-looking man. "We went all the way to the top!"

Praveen's family also subscribed to the modern notion of feeding their guests lots of little snacks instead of sitting them down to a proper, three-hour meal.

"Have some pakoras," Praveen's mother said reluctantly, holding a tray of pakoras in front of Younguncle and two other guests. She glared at him.

He took three pakoras and said, "Thank you," politely. His hostess stared at him in astonishment and then at the tray in dismay. Evidently

Younguncle had violated some unwritten rule to
the effect of one pakora per person. The other
two guests, seeing the expression on her face,

took a tiny pakora each, smiling uncertainly.

"Lovely pakoras," Younguncle said indistinctly, following Praveen's mother. "I must compliment the cook. Where's the kitchen?"

He helped himself to two more pakoras, smiling gently all the while, and followed her into the kitchen.

"Please, go away," Praveen's mother said desperately. Their cook was cutting tiny cucumber sandwiches in quarters and putting them on a serving tray.

"Ah, *Khansama*," Younguncle said, patting the cook on his shoulder. "Your pakoras are a dream. Go meet your public, my man. Hear them sing your praises. I will commence dissecting these sandwiches to the subatomic level. The guests can breathe them in. We'll spare them the trouble of chewing." He handed the startled cook a tray of pakoras that was lying on the counter, and pushed him out of the kitchen.

Before his angry hostess could say a word, Younguncle seemed to undergo one of his terrifying transformations. He metamorphosed from a smoothly courteous, charming young man, into a maniac. Brandishing a cucumber sandwich, he began leaping, grimacing, and hooting. He opened the door of the storeroom and began pouring rice into the lentil bin and dried beans into the rice bin, giggling, drooling, and rolling his eyes. When Praveen's mother bristled up to him, snarling, with an enormous wooden rolling pin in her hands, he whirled around so suddenly that she yelped. All her bravado disappeared.

"Help! *Koi hai?* Is anyone there? Come quick!"

Her husband came bustling in, looking irritated. Younguncle ran up to him with a low

howl and tried to feed him a cucumber sandwich. Praveen's father managed to fend him off
and yelled for help.

But the conversations in the other rooms
and the multiple TVs blaring drowned out his
voice. A few people who were nearby came drift-
ing into the kitchen, wondering what was going
on. As they did, Younguncle emerged with the
tray of tiny sandwiches.

"Please, have some," he said politely. "These
are quite delicious little treats. From France,
you know. From the land of the Eiffel Tower
and other tall tales!"

People smiled, thinking, what an amusing,
obliging young man.

Later, Praveen's father drew an acquaintance
aside.

"That young fellow, what does everyone call
him? Younguncle? Is he normal?"

The acquaintance, who knew Younguncle's family well and was a bit of a philosopher, said, "Normal? Good heavens! Definitely not. A Special Edition, that is Younguncle. Normal? What an idea!"

"Is it true he was once kidnapped by a troop of monkeys?"

"Oh, you've heard that story? Yes, when he was a baby. The monkeys near the Govindpur temple took off with him. They tossed him around but didn't harm him. Apparently he had a whale of a time. But it was quite long ago. Who told you about that?"

"My daughter-in-law-to-be."

"Yes, Younguncle has been a celebrity at various times in his life, starting with that event. A very nice young man, I must say."

Praveen's father trembled with fury.

"He's dangerous! He attacked me in the

kitchen just now! He tried to choke me with a sandwich! He tried to bite my ear!"

Which, of course, Younguncle had not done, having far better taste than that, not to mention a sense of hygiene.

His acquaintance shook his head.

"He couldn't have, my dear sir. You must be mistaken. I've known that family for decades. Younguncle is a strict vegetarian."

The next day, Younguncle's parents received a note from Praveen's parents. It said that the family astrologer had redone the horoscopes for the wedding and found that the match was inauspicious, after all. So the wedding was off.

Rekha burst into tears of relief. Her mother, misunderstanding, patted her on her back, her own eyes filling with angry tears. Her husband walked up and down the room, growling insults.

"Horoscope-shoroscope! What liars! I happen to know that several of our friends have been told by those people that insanity runs in our family! Rumor-mongers! Rotten pakoras! Insanity? Ha! I'll give them insanity!"

Younguncle looked innocently around at his family. Rekha peered at him from between her fingers. He thought she was smiling through her tears.

"It is a good thing," said his mother thoughtfully, "that people in this town know us, and those people are just newcomers. Otherwise everyone would have wondered what was so wrong with the girl that the engagement was being broken. Don't cry, Rekhoo, *bachhi*, all will be well. There are plenty of other families lining up with their young men! We'll find another Boy for you!"

"And did they?" Sarita asked, when Younguncle told them all this upon his return.

"Not yet," Younguncle said. "Your aunt Rekha has become very fussy. She finds fault with all the young men who come hopefully to the door with their parents, and when they have been reduced to a sufficiently nervous state, she tells them the joke of the snake charmer's mother-in-law and the camel. So far she has found no one who truly appreciates it. But surely it is only a matter of time!"

Younguncle
and the
Monkey Summer

Younguncle's first summer in his new home brought with it a heatwave so terrible that the trees all shriveled up, the ground became cracked and dusty, and the grass in the playground looked like old people's hair. It was bad enough that water was rationed in the summer as a matter of course, but now the water supply was cut down to two hours a day. Two hours a day! That meant no long, lazy cool baths to wash off the dust and sweat, and no running the desert-cooler fan for more than an hour or two. Younguncle's sister-in-law, normally a cheerful, efficient, managerial sort of person, grumbled all day long. Her children grew listless because the moment they stepped outside they felt as though they were in a furnace. The electricity supply did not oblige them more than a few hours a day, so that most often Younguncle and his young charges sat in a stupor, sipping fresh limewater and falling asleep over their games of Snakes and Ladders.

There came a day when the heat was so intense that the sun drank up all the water in the streams and pools of the forest outside the town. Troops of thirsty monkeys came into town to eat fruit and steal whatever little water was used for vegetable gardens. Although people were afraid of the monkeys, they also considered them to be sacred, so rather than driving them away, mostly they just kept their children inside and let the monkeys be.

In due time, a troop of monkeys settled down in the guava trees of Younguncle's back garden. They seemed happy enough there and did not interfere with the family, although Younguncle's sister-in-law entreated him to keep an eye on the children. Younguncle himself, everyone knew, was unlikely to be the target of monkey mischief. He had been kidnapped as a child by the monkeys of Govindpur temple and returned safely to his family after a wild joyride among the trees, so people knew that the monkey god Hanuman had especially blessed him. Sometimes neighbors came and asked if Younguncle would intercede with the monkeys on their behalf, but Younguncle always politely refused.

"There is a higher purpose behind their presence, Auntie," he would say, setting iced lime-water before his elderly guest. "Who am I to interfere with the cosmic drama? Stay inside, keep the little ones with you, and remember Hanuman. All will be well."

And the neighbor would leave after a while, inexplicably comforted, and tell everyone what a fine young fellow Younguncle was.

Now although the heat had adversely affected the enterprise and energy levels of the two older children, the baby was just as usual. She spent her spare time crawling about the house, pulling herself up along a sofa or chair, waiting for Younguncle to relax his guard. The baby's chief ambition in life was to find and consume an entire shirt of Younguncle's, and Younguncle knew this. Although they loved each other very much, Younguncle and the baby had completely different ideas on the meaning and purpose of shirts. And one day the baby got her chance.

Younguncle liked to leave his shirts out to cool after he had ironed and folded them, because he hated wearing hot shirts that smelled of the close confines of the wooden cupboard. So he would air his ironed shirts on the bed or the table, all the while keeping a wary eye on the baby. Lately he had found a new hiding place, and since the baby could not crawl as fast as Younguncle could walk, this place was still a secret. It made the baby quite furious.

One day, she happened to be sitting under the dining table, musing on strategy, when Younguncle crept in stealthily. He went to the fridge (the baby was by now peering out from under the table), opened the freezer, and took out several shirts, all neatly ironed and folded. Looking about him like a criminal, he was making his way out when the phone rang in the next room. "Younguncle, phone!" shouted his sister-in-law from the kitchen. Younguncle looked about wildly, put his shirts on the table, and ran off to answer the phone.

The baby emerged, grabbed a shirt off the stack (it was deliciously cool), and brandished it triumphantly. Just as she began to chew, she saw that she was no longer alone.

A strange, wizened, hairy face was looking in through the window with an air of great interest.

The hairy face had such beautiful, pleading brown eyes! As she chewed on the shirt, it occurred to the baby that the shirt was (in this instance) better used for a higher purpose. She went to the window and pushed the shirt through the iron grillwork. The monkey inclined its head in a curiously polite manner, put its hands delicately on the shirt, and pulled. It fondled the shirt (still cool from its sojourn in the freezer) and chattered to the baby in a pleased sort of way. Then suddenly it bounded off.

We will not dwell on what happened after Younguncle returned to the dining room. Suffice it to say that when his nice white shirt was found to be missing from the stack and the baby was found in the same room with an incredibly smug expression on her plump face, there was consternation in the household.

There were visits from the doctor and a discussion of the baby's potty contents and much worrying and administering of herbal remedies, through all of which the baby remained quite serene. After a couple of days the family realized that if the baby had indeed eaten the shirt, her digestive system must have been robust enough to completely absorb it.

On the third day after the baby's alleged

consumption of the shirt, Younguncle's sister-in-law, the baby's mother, had a fright. She had been lying down in her upstairs bedroom in the hot, still evening, fanning herself with a hand-held *punkha*, when she saw a ghost.

It was sitting on the mango tree outside the window. It was all in white. It seemed to be reading a book.

Sister-in-Law screamed. The cook, the washerwoman, and the family dropped whatever they were doing and came running. She pointed with a trembling finger at the window, but the apparition had disappeared.

"Don't worry, Sister-in-Law," Younguncle said soothingly. "If it is afraid of your scream, it has some sense. It won't come back."

The washerwoman shook her head and started on a lurid story of how her mother-in-law was kidnapped by a ghost.

"Nonsense," Younguncle's elder brother interrupted. "It is the heat. You must have imagined it."

His wife fixed him with a firm eye. Her habit of speaking in words that began with Capital Letters made most people nervous.

"I Did Not Imagine It," she said. And that was that.

The children, excited, stayed and watched for the ghost, but it did not return.

"Have you seen my book?" Younguncle asked Sarita and Ravi the next morning. "I left it lying on the cot in the courtyard yesterday. It has completely disappeared."

He looked suspiciously at the baby, who returned an indignant glance. Books were at the moment beneath her notice. Besides they did not, as a rule, taste very nice.

The ghost appeared again three nights later.

This time Sister-in-Law did not scream. She went silently from the room, got the family, and pointed out the apparition.

"Seems to be a well-behaved sort of ghost," Younguncle said. "Perhaps we should just let it be."

It truly was a strange summer: the intense heat, the monkeys, the disappearance of the shirt, the missing book (which by the way was called *Life Experiences of a Wandering Mendicant* by one Swami Nenua Laal). The strangeness did not stop at that, however, because the next morning Ramu the milkman came running down the street, near tears, shouting that his cow, his delight, his livelihood, his precious Janaki, was missing.

Everyone in the neighborhood knew Ramu and Janaki. They would come to the front gate of every house in the early morning, and a child or servant would run out with a pail. Ramu would look apologetically at the cow and tie her hind legs with a cloth, all the while singing to her in a truly awful monotone. The cow would eat grass from a little cloth bag, while trying to shut out the sound of Ramu's singing. Milk would splash merrily into the pail. Ramu always had to be watched while he was milking the cow because otherwise he would mix water in the milk. He wore a ragged shawl that (according to gossip) hid a large and dirty bottle of water. Once Younguncle had offered him a bottle of nice, clean water to make his job simpler, resulting in a flood of histrionics from Ramu, which fortunately ended in companionable laughter. But most of the time Sarita and Ravi performed the duty of supervising the milking.

"Why don't you two children run off and let

a poor man do his job?" Ramu would say. "You are making my cow nervous."

"It's not us, it's your singing," Sarita would reply. "Besides if we go away you'll water down the milk."

Ramu would look at her with a hurt expression on his face, his perpetually sad eyes brimming with tears.

"Ah, a poor man must bear the insults of those he serves," he would sigh.

But on this day Ramu was truly distraught. People came out of their houses, and soon a large crowd was gathered about him.

"How did you lose her, Ramu?" someone asked.

"You know how it is, sir," Ramu said, taking off his turban and drying his face with it. "After the morning round I let her roam around to graze. She comes home in the evening on her own. Likes routine, Janaki does. When I am late getting up in the mornings she sticks her face in the window of my hut and moos at me. Well, last evening she didn't come home at all."

He began sobbing again.

"She's the best milking cow I have ever had! The sweetest, the gentlest! Her milk is the best in all of town! Oh calamity!"

After everyone had promised to look for Janaki, Ramu left, a pitiful, broken man. Sarita found her own eyes filled with tears.

"We *must* find Janaki, Younguncle," she said. Younguncle looked thoughtful and nodded.

Days passed and there was still no sign of Janaki. Ramu borrowed a cow from a distant relative and continued on his rounds, but the cow was bad-tempered and almost gored Ramu with her large, curving horns. His nephew had to accompany him every morning to help control the cow. Ramu did not sing anymore. Instead he wept and groaned about how much he missed Janaki. Everyone felt sorry for him, although they did not miss his singing. The children and Younguncle had gone searching for Janaki everywhere, to no avail.

Younguncle had, in the meantime, made friends with the monkeys living in the back garden. Some of the monkeys in other gardens had been destructive, breaking branches, pulling out saplings, running wild, and showing their teeth, but these monkeys did nothing of the sort. Younguncle, with his sister-in-law's approval, offered them small gifts of fruit and water every day.

One day, the children and Younguncle went to the tennis club to look for tennis balls. This club was in a nearby, affluent neighborhood where nearly every house had an air conditioner. The club had been built by the corrupt merchant Paytu Lal, who charged the members exorbitant fees so that they could look down on other people not as privileged as they. Once, Younguncle had discovered two tennis balls lying in a ditch by the road in front of the club. He had tried to return them to the guard at the gate, but the guard had shouted at him instead.

"I know you people, trying to get into the grounds any way you can," the guard had said. "This is a *pry-wate* club, very *pry-wate*. The likes of you can get lost."

After that, Younguncle pocketed any tennis balls that he found lying outside the club grounds.

The children found five tennis balls in various states of disrepair. They were thrilled. Younguncle had a plan, a very amusing one.

They walked quickly home. On the way they

passed a high-walled enclosure. From within it they could hear the sound of a water sprinkler. They could see the tops of fruit-bearing trees. The air smelled of ripening mangoes.

"What place is that, Younguncle?" Sarita asked.

"It is a private garden owned by one of Paytu Lal's cohorts," Younguncle said. "People say it is a veritable paradise. There is no water shortage there, and all the fruit goes directly to Paytu Lal's table."

They passed an iron gate in the wall. A man with a spade glared at them from behind the bars.

When they got home they went into the kitchen for some much needed limewater, and then they slipped into the back garden.

The monkeys were chattering sleepily among themselves in the guava trees. Younguncle and the children stood a little way from the trees, tossing the tennis balls to one another. Younguncle was holding the baby with one arm, and between them they did not miss a single catch. Meanwhile, the monkeys stopped chattering and began to watch in earnest.

Then, apparently by mistake, Younguncle threw the ball toward the trees. A brown, hairy arm reached nimbly for the ball and caught it.

Younguncle pretended not to notice.

The monkeys passed the ball around. Then one of them began tossing it into the air. Another monkey caught the ball and dropped it. Younguncle retrieved the ball and threw it up to the monkeys.

After that, the monkeys, the children, and Younguncle began to play the most wonderful game of catch ever. Five balls danced in the air, tossed from monkey to monkey to humans and back. None ever touched the ground. The game went on in utter silence, like a fantastic ballet. Then Sister-in-Law's stern voice broke the silence.

"What are you doing Outside in the Heat!" she shouted from the courtyard. "Come in At Once and Have Something to Drink."

The monkeys retreated. Disappointed, the children were turning away when Ravi noticed something. "Look!"

Up in the thickest part of the guava tree over his head, somebody was sitting, all in white, reading a book.

"The gh-gh-ghost!" Sarita said.

"Gah!" said the baby cheerfully.

They stood rooted to the spot. Then Young-uncle went carefully under the tree and looked up. He began to smile.

"It is not a ghost. It's a monkey," he said.

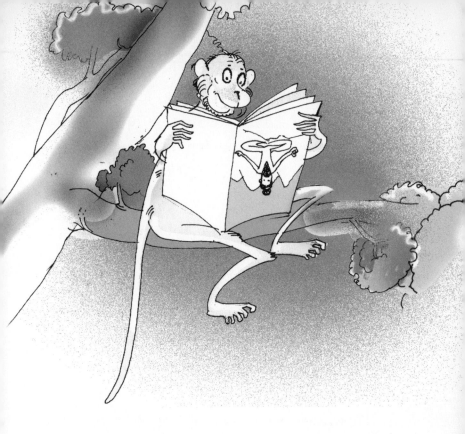

He shook his head at the baby, smiling. "It is
a monkey wearing my shirt and reading my
book, *Life Experiences of a Wandering Mendicant* by Swami Nenua Laal. Upside down."

"He didn't play catch with us, did he, that

monkey?" Sarita asked as they went into the house.

"I think he may be a little too dignified for that. Perhaps he is studying how to be human. He probably thought our little game was too monkeylike for him."

Over the next few days, Younguncle seemed rather preoccupied. The children wondered what was bothering him. He went about deep in thought. He disappeared for hours on end. They did play a few more games of catch with the monkeys, though, and it was only during these times that Younguncle seemed quite himself.

Then, one afternoon, Younguncle ushered the children into the drawing room, his finger on his lips. The household was having its siesta.

"I have found Ramu's cow," he whispered. "There is a problem, however. She needs to be rescued. I have a plan."

The children were thrilled. They listened very carefully to Younguncle.

The next morning they all woke early. After a quick breakfast they went into the back garden with the tennis balls. The sun had just risen, and the monkeys were awake and alert.

The game of catch began. But after a few minutes Younguncle gathered all the balls. He walked to the next tree. The monkeys leapt onto the branches of that tree and the game began again.

Then, slowly, Younguncle began to edge away from the trees. He walked along the garden wall, tossing balls in the air. Six or seven monkeys followed, including the one in the shirt.

A rather strange procession began making its way down the lanes of the neighborhood. There was Younguncle holding the baby, the two older children, and the monkeys following along, keeping to the tops of brick walls, venturing down to the ground where necessary. It was still early, and only a lone figure or two was visible in the distance. At last they reached the high-walled enclosure of Paytu Lal's private garden.

They did not go to the gate, but to the wall at the other end. The top of the ten-foot brick wall was encrusted with broken glass that had been stuck in the cement.

Younguncle fished out a spare bedcover from the cloth bag he had slung over his shoulder. It was folded several times and was quite thick. He flung it high up over the wall. The bedcover formed a soft padding on the top of the wall.

Then he took all five balls and flung them into Paytu Lal's garden.

The monkeys did not hesitate. Joyfully they

leapt up a nearby tree, jumped onto the top of the wall where the bedcover protected them from the sharp glass, and disappeared from view.

Younguncle gave the baby to Sarita and began to climb the tree that the monkeys had used to get onto the wall. Ravi jumped up and down in excitement. There were all kinds of noises coming from the other side of the wall.

This is what Younguncle saw:

The monkeys had discovered the ripe fruit in the garden. They had dropped the balls and were eating in a frenzy. The gardener rushed toward them, shouting and waving his rake. He saw a dirty tennis ball lying on the ground. In a rage, he picked it up and flung it at the monkeys.

The monkeys, not to be outdone, looked for something to throw back at the gardener, and all they had at hand was the fruit. They chased the gardener, pelting him with fruit. Only the silent, shirt-clad monkey did not participate. He sat by the fountain, reading his book (upside down). The gardener saw this astounding sight and screamed with anger. He tried to hit the solitary monkey with a bamboo pole, but before he could do that, the other monkeys had grabbed the end of the pole. The gardener dropped the pole and fled toward the gate.

He shot back the bolt and ran out into the street, yelling. As soon as he was around the corner, Younguncle slipped through the gate. He went swiftly to a grove of neem trees, where, tied to a stake, was Janaki. He undid the rope that bound her and led her out of Paytu Lal's garden.

The children hugged Janaki and led her toward their street. The monkeys, having eaten their fill, followed them at a leisurely pace. Younguncle retrieved the bedcover.

As they were leaving, they heard a shout behind them. The gardener had seen them. He began to run toward them, waving his stick.

"Run, children!" Younguncle said. As they and Janaki broke into a run, Younguncle started shouting in a terrified voice.

"Help! Help! A maniac is chasing us!"

Doors opened. People came pouring out of their houses. It was quite a procession, with Younguncle, the children, and Janaki in the lead, the gardener following, and people running to catch up with them to find out what was going on.

"Oh look, it's Janaki! And Younguncle and the children are with her!"

"Where did you find her, Younguncle?"

"Someone go tell Ramu!"

Defeated, the gardener stopped running. He glared balefully at the crowd around Younguncle, turned around, and slunk away. He knew when he was defeated.

And as they entered the lane where they lived, they saw Ramu running toward them, his turban askew. He was wailing.

"Janaki, my Janaki!" he sobbed, putting his arms around the cow's white neck.

Moo! said Janaki fondly, and licked the tears off his face.

More people were coming out of their houses to see what all the fuss was about. They crowded around Janaki and Ramu.

"Where did you find her, Younguncle?"

"Oh goodness, look at all those monkeys!"

"Who was that in a white shirt?"

Younguncle smiled and greeted everyone politely without quite answering anyone's questions. Quickly, he led the way home.

Later, the children learned that the gardener

had returned to the garden with Paytu Lal's henchmen, ready to beat and drive away all the monkeys. When they entered, they saw the place was in a shambles, with fruit littering the lawns, and the fountain askew. The monkeys had disappeared.

"Perhaps you imagined them. Maybe it was a bunch of neighborhood boys raiding the place while you were gone with the gate open," one of the toughs said scornfully.

The gardener was indignant.

"I tell you I saw them," he said. "They must have driven the cow onto the street. Monkeys are clever. There was even one dressed in a white shirt, reading a book by the fountain."

At this the three toughs laughed heartily.

"The heat has got to you, you fool!" they said. And that was that.

The monkeys did not stay all summer. Younguncle's friend Yusuf, a wildlife expert, began a project to restore the water supply to the forest. In a small clearing in the jungle, Yusuf had a well dug and topped with a hand-pump. The monkeys learned to use this in no time, and the pool of water around the pump was enough for all those other forest creatures not blessed with opposable thumbs.

After Janaki's return, Younguncle's neighborhood settled back to its usual pace, but with one difference. Everyone kept an eye on Janaki's whereabouts. They did not want her to disappear again. Ramu liked to exaggerate about a lot of things, but he was right about one thing: Janaki produced the best, tastiest, richest milk in town.

Younguncle's
Village Visit

Summer had been washed away by the monsoons, and after a month of steady rain, the clouds receded to make way for the cooler season. Younguncle began planning another trip, this time to his father's village, where he had spent some memorable summers as a schoolboy. Most of his family had moved out of the ancestral village home and spread over the cities and small towns of northern India, but two of his oldest relatives still lived in the village. These were Ancient Uncle and his wife,

Ancient Auntie. Ancient Uncle was Younguncle's great-uncle, but most people called him Ancient Uncle because he was very old. Whenever they mentioned him they would say, "Oh, Ancient Uncle!" and shake their heads, because he often didn't behave like a dignified old man of eighty-eight. In fact Sarita's last memory of him, during one of his rare visits to their town, involved crawling with him on hands and knees under the dining table to scare the dinner guests. Ancient Uncle had horses and cows, and there were plenty of family stories about their exploits. The children really wanted to go with Younguncle to see their legendary relative, but their mother put her foot down.

"What! Go see Ancient Uncle without Me to keep you all out of Mischief? Certainly Not!"

"But Younguncle will be there!" said Ravi.

"Younguncle Plus Ancient Uncle Means Even

More Trouble!" their mother said grimly. "And what about School?"

The children were disappointed. Younguncle reminded them that this trip would bear fruit in new stories, but they wouldn't smile. He told them three hair-raising old stories about the demon Gobarmal, which cheered them up only a little. This was surprising, because the Gobarmal stories were part of the family tradition, and the children loved being terrified by them.

"What long faces!" Younguncle said finally. "All right, never mind Gobarmal and his seven eyes. Tell me what you want from the village, apart from the usual fine crop of tall tales, and I'll be sure to bring it for you."

The two older children looked happier. They decided they wanted mangoes more than anything, because the village mangoes were the best in the known universe. They grew only in special groves near the village, and were large, golden, luscious, and ambrosial, enough to inspire poetry in the most prosaic soul. But the baby, being more ambitious than her siblings, wasn't satisfied with mere fruit. She frowned and pondered.

The next day, Younguncle's friend Yusuf came to visit. He was a wildlife expert who could make the most amazing animal noises, and he always liked to entertain the children. This time he brought them a picture book full of all kinds of animals. After doing his mandatory imitation of a hoolock gibbon in full howl, he turned to Younguncle with a worried look.

"I'm very worried about the Neelamgiri National Sanctuary," he said. "It is a small, protected forest, one of the last resorts of the Indian tiger. But each forest ranger I appoint to look after it leaves after a week or so and will not tell me why."

He paused to imitate a dyspeptic water buffalo, then, after the children's giggles had subsided, he became gloomy again.

"I don't know what the trouble is, and unfortunately I don't have time to visit Neelamgiri. . . . But listen—it's not too far from your village. Could you look into it for me, my friend?"

Younguncle enthusiastically agreed. Later, when he was showing the baby the animal book, she pointed at a picture of a tiger reposing royally in a forest clearing.

"Deh!" she said imperiously.

"I can't bring you a whole tiger," Younguncle said. "They won't allow him on the bus."

The baby looked thoughtful. Then she pointed at the tiger's tail.

"Deh!" she said with a magnanimous air.

"I can't bring you a tiger's tail, either," Young-uncle said. "The tiger might object."

The baby looked impatient. Then she pointed to the very tip of the tiger's tail.

"A hair from the tip of the tiger's tail? Well . . . I'll try my best," promised Younguncle. He didn't know how he was going to do it, especially if the hair was still attached to the tiger, but a promise was a promise.

So two days later, Younguncle waved good-bye to his brother and sister-in-law and the three children, and took a rickshaw to the bus stand. He put his suitcase on the roof of the bus, making sure to tie it down with some rope, and settled down in his seat to read his favorite book, *Life Experiences of a Wandering Mendicant* by Swami Nenua Laal. The bus soon filled with people. There were people on the seats, people in the aisle, people on the rooftop with the luggage, and people poking out of doors and windows. There were also people clinging to the ladder at the back of the bus that allowed access to the roof, but the driver, a young man with a beard and a tragic air, chased them off. The bus started with a great belch and a lurch, nearly dropping the passengers on the roof, and they were off.

The bus rumbled through the untidy neighborhoods and crowded streets of the town and emerged into the countryside. The fields were yellow with mustard flowers as far as the eye could see, and here and there were dark smudges of mango groves. Water gleamed in narrow canals where children bathed and splashed, and little thatched-hut villages appeared like mushrooms in the midst of the fields and disappeared in a flash as the bus sped past at about sixty miles an hour.

"At this rate, we will get to our destination yesterday," Younguncle said, shutting his book. People around him nodded and smiled.

"This driver, Ram Lakhan, he drives like a maniac," someone said. "Someone once told him if he drove fast enough he could go back in time, and he has been trying ever since."

"But why does he want to go back in time?"

"They say he saw a young woman at a fair, eating a golden mango that was exactly the color of her skin, and fell in love with her. The story goes that she looked at him and dropped one of her mangoes from her basket. It rolled to his feet, but in the excitement of trying to grab it at the same time as a street urchin, a clerk, and a fat woman selling rolling pins, he lost sight of her. He thinks if he could go back in time, he could track her down and ask her to marry him. So he's always in a hurry. Ten people have to shout in his ear to get him to stop the bus. You'd think he'd have some sense—by now his beloved is probably married with three children and four chins—but he doesn't give up."

There was general laughter.

"You look like a likely fellow," an elderly man said to Younguncle. "Not married, are you? My brother's daughter is of marriageable age. What caste are you from?"

Now the word for caste in Hindi, *jaati*, is the

same as one of the words for race, so the man's question sounded just like: "What race are you from?"

"I'm from the human race," Younguncle said politely. "And you?"

People laughed.

"A wit, a wit!" said an old lady. "He looks well turned-out and educated, obviously upper caste. You should snap him up for your niece without asking foolish questions."

"Er . . . my sister-in-law is already making arrangements. . . ." Younguncle said hurriedly. He was afraid he might find himself engaged by the end of the journey. The prospect of marriage was one of his recurring nightmares. "Besides, Auntie, I have spiritual leanings," he said, showing her the cover of his book, on which a hairy man in orange robes grinned against a backdrop of snowy mountains. "Marriage is not for those of us blessed with contemplative natures. I am thinking of retiring to the Himalayas. . . ."

The bus went over a bump in the road, and the passengers were, for a moment, airborne. Miraculously the luggage and the passengers on the roof stayed intact despite the brief moment of levitation. A woman screamed. A man near Younguncle grumbled.

"That idiot, Ram Lakhan! If only *he* would retire to the Himalayas!"

"He has never had an accident yet. Don't worry!" said the man with the marriageable niece.

By the end of the journey, the passengers had gotten to know one another quite well. Younguncle knew the names of their children, the chief eccentricities of their in-laws, and who was getting married to whom. When the bus approached the stop for his village, he felt almost reluctant to leave his new friends. The driver showed no signs of stopping, so half the bus had to stand up and yell, "Stop! Stop!" There was a tremendous screech of brakes, and the bus slowed down, raising a cloud of dust. Coughing, Younguncle took a running leap out of the doorway. When he could see again, there was Ancient Uncle, looking as thin and bony and sprightly as ever, sitting in the bullock cart, his mouth full of mango. Ancient Uncle stood up on the cart and yelled at the bus, now fast disappearing down the road.

"Your luggage, my boy! The bus is taking off with your luggage! Hop on!"

Younguncle hopped onto the cart. Ancient Uncle clapped his hands and the bullock sped forward like a rocket. Young-uncle found himself clutching the edge of the cart for dear life.

"Greetings, Ancient Uncle," he panted. "You have a very fast bullock."

"Ah yes," Ancient Uncle said, leaning forward in the excitement of the charge. "Bira here was brought up with my horse, Hira. He thinks he's a horse, and a racehorse at that. Come on, Bira, you slowpoke, catch that bus!"

Younguncle stood up precariously and yelled and waved at the bus to stop. The bus passengers, especially the ones on the roof, thought this was great

fun. They yelled and waved back. Bira moved like a great, humped mountain, streaks of dust and sweat gathering on his white flanks.

The bus passengers kept cheering on the bullock cart, which was gradually catching up with the bus. Suddenly, the man with the marriageable niece had a thought.

"Maybe he changed his mind! Maybe he does want to marry my niece! Stop the bus!"

The passengers took up the cry.

"Stop the bus! In the name of the human race, stop the bus!"

For the second time the bus ground to a dramatic halt. Younguncle leapt off the cart, swarmed up the ladder at the back of the bus, and retrieved his suitcase. He got back on the road and waved his thanks.

"Good-bye, uncles and aunts and friends! May you have a safe journey!"

"Wasn't that fun!" Ancient Uncle said, grinning. He had lost a few teeth since Younguncle had seen him last. "Nothing like a good chase to build up the bones."

Younguncle could not help but agree. They took the long way back, over dusty village tracks through fields of sunflowers and mustard, to where the old house stood dreaming by the riverbank.

Ancient Auntie was waiting in the front veranda of the house, her face wreathed in smiles. She frowned at her husband.

"What have you done with the boy? He's covered with dust! Let Bandhu take care of Bira—you both need to wash up and eat."

Younguncle couldn't help noticing that the whitewash was peeling off the walls of the house. It was obsessively neat and clean, but the sofa cover was threadbare and the curtains almost worn through with many washings. The legendary stables were empty, except for Hira and Bira. His great-uncle and great-aunt were both wrinkled with age, and so was the cook, Bandhu. They all seemed smaller and more bent and tired than he remembered from his school days, when he had visited them in the summers.

But Hira was a beautiful horse. Ancient Uncle showed Younguncle proudly around the stables and introduced his pride and joy. Hira's coat and mane were a striking reddish-brown, and in the sunlight he glowed with a copper tint. Ancient Uncle spent half the day grooming him and describing all his virtues to Younguncle. "He's the fastest horse in the world, I think," Ancient Uncle said. At this, Bira let out an indignant moo.

"All right, all right, you are the fastest bull

in the world, you slowpoke!" Ancient Uncle said, patting Bira affectionately. "He's jealous," Ancient Uncle whispered to Younguncle. "Loves Hira like a brother, but wants exactly the same amount of praise and attention, or he'll sulk for days."

Later, after a meal that made him feel like a water buffalo, Younguncle staggered out into the pleasant evening. The sun was setting over the Neelam River, which was small and serpentine, but very swift. A huge banyan tree stood at the edge of the bank, its multiple trunks creating a profusion of leafy rooms. A childhood memory stirred in Younguncle's mind.

"I wonder if the ghost is still in the tree," he said to himself.

He went up to the nearest trunk of the tree and tapped on it. Immediately a low, quavering moan wafted through the air.

"Giiiive me myyyy money!"

There was an ominous cracking of twigs and small branches overhead.

Younguncle smiled. Some things never changed.

"I am a child of this house, sir," he said politely. "I am not the one who owes you." The ghost stopped moaning, and a shower of leaves descended softly around Younguncle.

At night, when Younguncle's cot had been set up next to Ancient Uncle's on the rooftop, and the mosquito netting arranged around it, Younguncle asked Ancient Uncle to remind him about the ghost's story. He lay under the netting, watching the moon rise and the stars glitter in the vast sky above him. A cool breeze wafted from the river.

"Ah, yes," Ancient Uncle said sleepily. "It was in the time of my father that the ghost began to haunt the tree. A man called Bakvaasnath used to live in a hut under the tree—he was some relation of my mother's family, and they say he was of a spiritual nature. Despite this he had managed to save up quite a sum of money that he kept in a box by his bed. Now not far from here lives the clan of that rascal of a landlord, Gobarmal—who, if there is any justice in the universe, has surely been reborn as a cockroach. Gobarmal's cousin cheated Bakvaasnath into lending him quite a bit of money for some fraudulent scheme. He told Bakvaasnath he would be back in a few days by riverboat. So Bakvaasnath waited all day and night by the riverbank. . . ."

A night bird called. The wind dropped suddenly, but the leaves of the banyan tree rustled as though someone else was sitting in the branches, listening to the story.

" . . . and one day he was mildly surprised to find that he had left his body lying inside the hut. People came and performed the funeral rites but he didn't care. All he wanted was his money back. He kept waiting for Gobarmal's cousin's boat to return over the water with his money. Poor fellow, he is waiting still."

A thought occurred to Younguncle.

"This Gobarmal," he said. "We tell stories of a demon called Gobarmal at home. I think I heard them first from Father. Is it possible . . . ?"

"The very same scoundrel," Ancient Uncle said, sitting up and shaking his fist. "Gobarmal senior died when I was a boy, but his eldest son, also called Gobarmal, is his spitting image. This Gobarmal junior is now head of the clan, and they say he is even more powerful and depraved than his father. The clan is notorious in the whole district for the terrible things they have done. There is hardly a mother in the area who does not frighten her children into obedience by invoking the dreaded name of Gobarmal. Your father was brought up to fear the name—no wonder it is a family legend! Gobarmal's minions are spread everywhere. Why, only last year I sold my horses and the last two cows at the district fair—and I found out later that the man I'd sold them to was one of those wretched people! He had cheated me, naturally. It runs in their blood. Now they're after Hira, because he's the fastest horse in the world. But I will never part with Hira! Never!"

"Of course not," Younguncle said soothingly.

"Only two days ago they sent one of their ruffians to bargain with me. As though Hira's worth can be measured in rupees! I sent him off all right!"

He chuckled at the memory.

"And where do these lovely people live?" asked Younguncle.

"In the village of Neelamgiri. They own it, even though they are not supposed to, by law. They own the police, the landlords, even the bandits who haunt the roads. They take what they want, the scoundrels."

"Neelamgiri? Isn't there a national wildlife sanctuary there?" said Younguncle, remembering what his friend Yusuf had said.

"Sanctuary-banctuary!" Ancient Uncle said scornfully. "It is used by the Gobarmal clan as their private hunting ground, and nobody can stop them. There is an old tiger there they have been trying to catch for years. I wish he'd turn into a man-eater and gobble up the lot of them, but he's too civilized. Or has better taste. Do you know, there is a room in their mansion, or so I have heard, that is filled with the heads of all the animals they have killed in that forest? Deer, bears, panthers, and probably a tiger or two, I shouldn't wonder."

"I see," Younguncle said thoughtfully. He realized that his village visit was going to be more interesting than he'd imagined.

The very next day, things started to happen. The day began innocently enough.

Ancient Uncle asked Younguncle to take Ancient Auntie to the sari shop in the nearest town.

"I don't like going that far, you know, and sari shops always bore me. How about it? I'll be fine here on my own."

Younguncle nodded.

"Of course I'll take Auntie," he said. "I love sari shops."

Auntie gave Ancient Uncle a suspicious look.

"You won't get up to any mischief, will you?"

she said doubtfully. "No taking Hira racing on the riverbank—you know you are no longer young."

"I would never dream of such a thing," Ancient Uncle said virtuously. But as he waved good-bye at the bus stop, he winked conspiratorially at Younguncle.

Younguncle and Ancient Auntie had a great time in town. They swept into sari shops, where fat shopkeepers seated them and served them cold drinks and unrolled acres of bright saris before them. They bargained with gusto and came away in triumph with four saris, two of which were Younguncle's gifts to Ancient Auntie. On the bus journey back, the bus driver was none other than the silent, tragic, speed maniac, Ram Lakhan. Some of Younguncle's fellow travelers from his earlier trip were on the bus and they greeted him cheerfully. "Look! It's the young man from the human race!" they said, and made room for him and Ancient Auntie.

But when Younguncle and Ancient Auntie got back to the village house, all was in an up-roar.

Ancient Uncle was stamping about the court-yard, waving his fist in the air and shouting, while the cook, Bandhu, led the bullock out to him. Ancient Uncle started to climb on to Bira's broad back, but Ancient Auntie grabbed his foot.

"Where on earth are you going? What's happened?"

All the bluster went out of Ancient Uncle. He looked suddenly old and tired.

"I . . . I took Hira to the fair in the next vil-lage. You know, just a short excursion. I tied him to a tree while I was looking around . . . just five minutes, it was. I turned back—and he was gone."

"Gone? In the middle of the fair? How is

that possible? Everyone knows Hira! Someone must have seen who took him!"

"I asked," Ancient Uncle said despairingly.
"What do you think I've been doing for the past
three hours? I asked almost everyone in the
area, and they all denied seeing Hira being rid-
den off by someone else. I think they are lying.
I think they are afraid to say who it was. . . ."

"Now don't start that," Ancient Auntie said.
"If you'd only listened to me and stayed home
quietly and behaved yourself, this would never
have happened!"

"This was bound to happen," Ancient Uncle
said darkly. "You know how much the Gobarmal
clan wants Hira, and now they've—"

"We don't have proof," Ancient Auntie said.
Ancient Uncle climbed on to Bira's back, looking stubborn. "And where do you think you are
going? Get off Bira this instant! I will not let
you go to your death!"

"I have to confront them," Ancient Uncle said. "Hira is like a son to me—"

"You are a foolish old man, and I am not letting you go! Younguncle, stop him!"

Younguncle stood before Bira and helped ease Ancient Uncle off the bullock's back.

The old man was trembling with rage.

"Now you go and rest, Ancient Uncle," Younguncle said. "Leave it to me. I'll find out what is going on."

"I don't want you to get in trouble, Younguncle," Ancient Auntie said, looking worried. "What do you mean to do? Those people are dangerous. . . ."

"Don't coddle him, Auntie," Ancient Uncle said, looking more cheerful. "This boy knows how to use his wits!"

The next day Younguncle went into town again and bought a hundred cheap, shiny bangles, bracelets and necklaces, as well as a dozen lipsticks and eyeliners. He returned home, had a good lunch of spinach-stuffed flat-breads with pickled boiled potatoes, and then changed into a long shirt and a dhoti. Ancient Uncle helped tie a turban around his head, while Auntie looked on with a frown.

"There, he looks just like a local," Ancient Uncle said approvingly.

Younguncle put the bangles, bracelets, and knickknacks into a sack and slung it over his shoulder. He waved good-bye to the two old people.

"I wish I was going with you," Ancient Uncle said wistfully. "An adventure is good for building up the bones."

"But they know you, Ancient Uncle, and they don't know me. Don't worry. I will be back tonight."

And he set off over the fields.

He took a long, circuitous route to the village of Neelamgiri. He did not want anyone to think that he had come from Ancient Uncle's village. He walked briskly past fields of golden mustard, through tiny, ramshackle villages, shouting his wares. People came running out of huts.

"Where are you from, bangle-seller?"

"I come from the town, and I bring the finest things."

Younguncle sold a few trinkets on the way, and asked a man laboring in a field: "I have heard that there is a great house in this vicinity. I would like to sell my bangles to the ladies of the house. Could you direct me, brother?"

The man straightened up and pointed.

"But be careful," he said. "If they don't like you, you may never see the sun rise again!"

At last Younguncle saw a great monstrosity

of a mansion sitting among the green and yellow fields. It was fluorescent pink and decorated with an embarrassment of turrets and little towers.

Hmm, thought Younguncle, *clearly the product of a disturbed mind.*

A long road led up to the mansion, and there were stables on one side, along with cowsheds and groves of mango trees. He noticed that the rooftop bristled with antennas.

Two men with rifles stopped him near the entrance. Younguncle put on his most innocent and vacuous look and showed them his wares. Behind the guards, a great archway led to the central courtyard of the house.

"Bangles, bangles and kohl! Trinkets and anklets for the sensitive soul!" shouted Younguncle at the top of his voice. The guards jumped.

"Stop that, you nearly deafened me!"

One of them pushed roughly at Younguncle but just then women's voices called from the windows of the mansion.

"Oh, let him in!"

"I could do with some bangles!"

"Me, too!"

Younguncle was ushered into the courtyard. It was paved with marble, and small ornamental trees grew at the four corners. An ornate fountain stood in the middle. Around the courtyard, the mansion rose up pinkly on three sides.

Younguncle exclaimed in wonder.

"How gracious is the house of Gobarmal," he said to nobody in particular. "Surely even the horses walk with shoes of gold on his estate! Alas, my wares are as nothing before this splendor."

Younguncle set up a little wooden stand and hung the bangles from it.

"All the latest styles in town, ladies!"

Within moments he was surrounded by a fluttering crowd of women—old ladies and giggling young women and girls, all bedecked so much with jewelry that Younguncle couldn't understand why they'd need more. They exclaimed and cried out over his wares, and tried on bangle after bangle. Younguncle was surprised to see how excited they were over his cheap trinkets, since all their heavy traditional jewelry seemed to be solid gold.

Through the chattering of the women he heard the hum of several TVs coming from the rooms around the courtyard. He glanced up and saw the balconies of the upper floors overlooking the courtyard bustling with children and people going in and out of what seemed to be countless rooms. Servants rushed about with dusting cloths and food trays. Obviously

Gobarmal's clan was both rich and populous.

The women seemed incapable of talking about anything other than jewelry. When Younguncle casually asked about how many horses and cattle the great Gobarmal possessed, he was greeted with blank stares or giggles. He was careful not to persist with his questions. The guards still stood sullenly at the gates, watching the commotion as the women bought most of Younguncle's wares.

At last he was done. An enormous old woman in a green sari told him: "Go to the kitchens at the back and get something to eat."

Younguncle bowed humbly. He made his way to the rear courtyard, where one of the cook's minions brought him pooris with vegetables, wrapped in a banana leaf. Younguncle squatted in a corner of the courtyard and ate. Nobody seemed inclined to talk to him.

Licking his fingers, he wandered off toward the back of the mansion. The stables were a little distance away, but he did not want to go directly to them in case someone was watching. So he stepped into a clump of jacaranda trees, beyond which he could see a well and a hand-pump.

To his surprise, he found a young woman squatting on her haunches in front of the hand-pump with a pile of dirty pots and pans before her. She was sullenly scrubbing them with wood ash. Younguncle saw with a shock that there was an iron ring around one of her ankles. A rope attached to the ring was tied around a nearby tree.

The young woman gave Younguncle a hostile look.

"Who're you?"

Younguncle put his palms together in greeting.

"Just a humble bangle-seller, sister, going my way."

He was puzzled by the woman. She was wearing a nice yellow sari, and there was a thin silver chain around her neck—so she was clearly not a servant. What was she doing, tied up like an animal, washing dishes?

"Would you like some bangles?"

She gave him a dangerous look.

"Would you like me to throw you into that well? What will I do with bangles, you fool!"

Younguncle looked down.

"Well, I thought you would prefer some of mine to that thing around your ankle."

Her anger gave way to a bitter laugh.

"You noticed? That is my punishment for putting sugar instead of salt in the master's mutton curry. Ha! It was worth it just to see his face!"

"You are a cook, then?"

"You really are an idiot, aren't you? I am a member of the Gobarmal family, brother, a poor relation, who does all the running around for the ladies of the house. It is always 'Ranu, do this,' and 'Ranu do that'!"

Her eyes filled with angry tears.

"Now they're going to marry me off to a bandit with whom they have made an alliance. The rogue took a fancy to me, apparently, and the wedding will be in three days. Ever since they told me that, I have been putting chilies in the sweet rice and sugar in the savory dishes and glue in the embroidered shoes of the ladies. If they don't change their minds, I will throw myself down that well!"

"We cannot have that," Younguncle said, alarmed. "Why don't I cut this rope and help you escape?"

"Are you mad? Where would I escape to? Everyone around here knows who I am. The villagers are so afraid of Gobarmal that they would give me away, even though he makes their lives miserable. The only chance I have to get away is after dark, but at sunset the servants will come and fetch me, and then I'll be in the house doing the sewing. Blast them! I hope Gobarmal falls off his new horse!"

"What new horse?" Younguncle asked carefully.

"Oh, some horse. They say it is the fastest horse in the world. Gobarmal and his son Babu have gone riding on it. Tomorrow morning they are going to take it into the forest to hunt. I hope the tiger eats them."

She started crying in earnest now.

"There is a donkey, a big, stupid, stubborn donkey I feed every day. They are taking him

119

into the forest tomorrow as bait for the tiger!"

She paused to wipe her tears, and said fiercely: "Nobody will stand up to them! The idiot villagers around here think Gobarmal has supernatural powers that protect him, so they do nothing while he takes their land and crops. But the only power he has is fear. That is how he rules people. Except me! I would die rather than submit to his will!"

Younguncle thought quickly.

"When are Gobarmal and his son going to the forest tomorrow?"

"I heard them say around dawn. Why?"

"Listen, sister, do not fret. I must go now, but I will return for you."

And he vanished quickly into the trees, leaving the woman shaking her head.

"Who does he think he is?" he heard her saying to herself.

Younguncle took a roundabout way home. He told Ancient Uncle and Ancient Auntie that he had reason to think that Gobarmal's men had stolen Hira, and that he had a plan, but more than that, he would not say.

He woke well before dawn the next morning, breakfasted, and went to the great banyan tree by the river.

"Giiiive me myyyy money," quavered the ghost. Twigs and small branches snapped above Younguncle's head.

"It is only your nephew, Uncle Bakvaasnath," Younguncle said into the darkness. "I have come to ask if I may have a stout stick. I intend to teach Gobarmal and his son a lesson."

There was silence. Then he heard a long, low sound, like a sigh, and a sharp crack, and a small branch that had been half broken off by lightning fell at Younguncle's feet. He picked it up.

"Thank you, Uncle Bakvaasnath!"

Younguncle went into the house and received the blessings of Ancient Uncle and Ancient Auntie.

"Be careful, my child," Ancient Auntie said to him in a trembling voice. "What will I say to your parents if something terrible befalls you? All this for a horse . . ."

"Not only for the horse, Auntie. Don't worry, I will only do something *really* foolish. They won't expect that, you see."

He tied the branch of the banyan tree around his waist, clambered up on to Bira's back, and, with a cheery wave, set off toward the distant forest.

Bira seemed to know what was afoot, because he ran like the wind. When they reached the forest, the eastern sky was just beginning to glow with predawn light. A broad dirt track led into the jungle, flanked by a sign that pro-claimed in faded letters: NEELAMGIRI WILD-LIFE SANCTUARY: NO HUNTING. The forest rose up into distant blue hills, and birds antic-ipated the dawn with a cacophony of sound.

Keeping to the shelter of bushes and trees, Younguncle found a bamboo thicket so tight and compact that he had trouble getting Bira into it. But at last he managed.

"Wait for me here, Bira," he said, patting the bullock's white neck. "I will come back soon."

Younguncle had already noticed fresh horse tracks leading up the dirt path. There were three sets of hoofprints, which meant that Gobarmal and his son were each riding a horse and leading the poor, doomed donkey. He followed the tracks carefully. The trees rose around him in dark columns, casting deep shadows in the pale light of morning. Here and there a dragonfly with gauzy wings was caught in a shaft of sunlight, and creepers of wild rose cascaded down the ancient trees.

Ahead of him, Younguncle suddenly heard a loud, peevish voice raised in complaint.

"I'm tired of dragging along this stupid donkey! Can't we just shoot it?"

The whining voice was cut short. Another voice, cold and hard, cut in.

"Quiet, you fool! You know the tiger prefers fresh meat."

Younguncle crept cautiously through the undergrowth. Thanks to his friend Yusuf, he had learned how to move soundlessly through a forest. Through the trees he saw a tall man with gray hair on a black horse, and behind him a plump young man was riding Hira. The young man, presumably the whiny Babu, dragged the donkey behind him on a rope. The two horses were loaded with packs of food. Young-uncle sniffed the air. *Hmmm. Chicken curry*, he thought.

Ahead of the riders, six pigeons with irides-cent wings pecked about on the path.

"Quiet now, try to shoot one," said Gobar-mal.

Younguncle picked up a stone and flung it against a tree trunk. The stone bounced off the trunk and crashed into a bush. Up flew the birds. Gobarmal cursed.

"What was that?" Babu said.

"Branch falling. Keep going, we'll find some-thing bigger to kill."

They carried on in this manner, going deeper and deeper into the forest while Young-uncle followed them in the undergrowth. Their going was slow because the donkey kept plant-ing its broad feet in the ground and refusing to budge. Babu had to dismount and push the donkey's substantial rump several times to get him to move. Being kicked twice by the beast did not improve the young man's temper.

"Why couldn't we have brought some servants?" he muttered. "Why do I have to do all the work?"

"Because I want my son to become a man, not remain a spoiled brat!" said Gobarmal between his teeth. Babu cringed and said no more.

Finally, they reached a large clearing. At one edge of the clearing there was an enormous pipal tree. Clustered under its vast canopy were a group of smaller trees and thick bushes, gathered like children at the feet of a giant. Gobarmal and Babu led their horses into this miniature forest and tethered them.

"Now take the donkey to the other side of the clearing."

"I don't want to! What if the tiger comes along while I'm tying it up?"

"I will be up in the pipal tree, keeping watch. If the tiger comes, I will shoot him. But he won't come yet. Don't forget, my son, I know this beast well. I have been after him for a long time. In the morning he likes to rest near a pool about a mile east of here, where tall rushes grow. It is impossible to see the tiger among the rushes, and the beast has the patience of an ox—he can lie there and hide for hours if he knows there are humans around. But now the tiger is getting too old to hunt so well, so he is likely to be hungry. If I know him, as soon as he hears the donkey bray, he will come . . . right into our trap, heh heh heh."

The young man dragged the donkey toward a tree on the other side of the clearing. The donkey let forth a loud, protesting bray as he tied it down. Babu cursed and slapped the animal, which promptly kicked him on the shin.

"Ow! Ow!" yelled Babu.

"Shut up and climb up this tree. Did you have the pit dug yesterday?"

Babu ran like a hare to the tree and clambered up it, almost falling off in his hurry.

Younguncle was hiding under the pipal tree. From his vantage point he could see part of the clearing, and he could easily make out where Gobarmal and Babu were sitting from the sound of Babu's frightened huffing and puffing.

"Calm down, you fool! What a coward I have for a son! Did you have the pit dug?"

"Yes, yes I did, Father. See, you can see where I had the servants lay twigs and thin branches over it. There, near the donkey's tree. If our shots miss the tiger, it will surely fall in!"

"There is no certainty of that. You made it too

small across the top, you idiot. How deep is it?"

"Deeper than a man is tall."

Younguncle crept up to where the horses were tied. It occurred to him that he could, perhaps, untie Hira and ride away on him like the wind, but the two men above would certainly see him escaping, and they had guns. Besides, he wanted to do more than just rescue Hira. As he crept closer to the horses, he smelled the curried chicken again, and what seemed like paneer cooked in spinach, not to mention rice with nuts and raisins. Suddenly he had an idea.

It took him a minute to relieve the horses of their food packs. Gobarmal and his tubby son obviously had huge appetites, because there seemed to be enough to feed a small army. Younguncle propped his banyan-tree stick against the pipal tree's vast trunk and crept away, lugging the bags of food on his back.

Remembering what Gobarmal had said about the tiger's daily routine, he headed east, until the forest opened up into a large clearing next to a pond. It was sunny, warm, and humid here. Wild ducks swam on the dark water, which was surrounded by a murmuring sea of rushes. An enormous tiger, apparently attracted by the donkey's bray, stood amongst the rushes, sniffing the air with the delicacy of a gourmet chef. He saw Younguncle at once, and stiffened. Careful not to make any sudden moves, Younguncle bowed deeply and said: "Greetings, Your Majesty. Lunch is now served."

The tiger, apparently unused to such courtesy, kept up his imitation of a marble statue while Younguncle unhurriedly began unpacking the food. Finding a convenient flat-topped rock projecting from the ground, he overturned on it all the containers of chicken curry, sumptuous rice pilaf, and creamy spinach paneer. Around the edges, he laid out an array of stuffed flatbreads and topped it off with a couple of legs of mutton cooked to perfection in a stew of tomatoes, onions, and garlic. Having set out this repast, Younguncle bowed and stepped back.

"Enjoy, Your Majesty." And away he slipped.

The tiger, convinced he was in a surreal dream, padded cautiously up to the food. He snapped up a leg of mutton. The flavors burst upon his tongue. The tiger licked his lips and bent to the feast, marveling that such wonders existed in the gastronomic world. More than anything, the spinach paneer seemed to have been concocted by some celestial cook especially for the tiger's palate. All that he had tasted before this banquet seemed crude by comparison.

Now while Younguncle had been fattening the tiger (on the principle that a full tiger is a safe tiger), Gobarmal and Babu were waiting up the pipal tree. Babu had been trembling so much with fear that his father, afraid that he would fall right off the tree, had tied a rope around his waist and looped it over a projecting stump on the trunk nearby. He had brought the rope along to truss the tiger's dead body and drag it behind his horse in triumph. It was a rather long and very thick rope, so its other end dangled down the trunk and was lost in the undergrowth.

Younguncle crept back to his hiding place under the same tree and pondered his next move. While he was thinking, he heard Babu's startled gasp in the high branches above him.

"Shut up," Gobarmal hissed. "Here he comes!"

And then Younguncle saw, through the gaps in the bushes, the great beast enter the clearing. The tiger walked slowly toward the donkey, who was braying defiantly. The tiger gave a prolonged belch, turned away, skirted the twig-covered pit carefully, and went toward the very tree on which Gobarmal and Babu were hiding.

"Aim and shoot, you twit!" came Gobarmal's exasperated whisper.

But before Babu could do anything, the tiger had crawled into the coolness of the undergrowth and lain down with a deep sigh. He could smell Younguncle not three paces away, but after that wonderful meal, he was prepared to trust Younguncle for life. He could also smell the horses and the donkey, but he had eaten more than enough for the moment.

Meanwhile, Younguncle remembered his promise to the baby.

He crept into the shelter of a queen-of-the-night bush that (he hoped) hid his scent with the fragrance of its flowers. From here he could see the tiger's tail, twitching to and fro. He stretched his arm, carefully selected a single hair from the tip of the tiger's tail . . . and pulled.

The tiger didn't seem to notice. Younguncle breathed again, and put the hair in his shirt pocket. Above him, Babu was whispering frantically.

"How can we shoot him now? What about the horses?"

"We'll wait till he comes out of the bushes. Now shut up!"

It occurred to Younguncle that the tiger was

safest under the tree where his would-be kil-
lers were waiting. But how could he make sure
the tiger would stay put? He began to look

around him for a length of tough vine.

It was then that he saw Gobarmal's rope gathered in loops and folds around the base of the tree trunk.

Not realizing that the other end of the rope was tied around Babu's plump waist, Younguncle took the free end of the rope, eased back into the bushes, and tied it carefully around the tiger's tail.

The tiger was asleep, dreaming sweet dreams of smiling humans serving him vast vats of spinach paneer. Feeling a sudden tug on his tail, he leapt up with a growl, startling Younguncle, who climbed nimbly up a young gulmohur tree. The tiger ran around the undergrowth, roaring and swishing his tail. The rope became taut, the stump it was wrapped around broke with a sharp crack, and down came Babu, with a terrific yell. The tiger, terrified, burst into the open clearing, dragging Babu behind him on the rope. Babu, gibbering in fear, got to his feet and began to run in the opposite direction. As he was still attached to the tiger, they ended up chasing each other in a large circle around the clearing while Gobarmal cursed, shouted instructions, and tried to aim.

"Stay still, you idiot! I'm trying to shoot him!"

Suddenly there was a crash and a loud cry from Babu. The terrified young man had disappeared into the ground. He had crashed through the thin layer of leafy twigs over the pit and fallen into the pit himself! The donkey let out a loud, appreciative *hee-haw*. Meanwhile, the sudden jerk had pulled the rope off the tiger's tail, and the tiger, deciding enough was enough, bounded away into the forest.

Gobarmal started to climb down from the tree, fuming and cursing. Younguncle, quite stunned by the sudden turn of events, was still perched on the gulmohur tree. But before he could do anything, a large branch snapped and fell from the pipal tree above Gobarmal, hitting him heavily on the head. Gobarmal lost his grip, crashed down through the branches, and landed at the bottom with a thunk.

A familiar quaver filled the air.

"Giiiive me myyy money!"

The ghost!

Bakvaasnath must have hitched a ride on the branch that Younguncle had brought along from the old banyan tree. The thought of revenge had probably been too much for the ghost to resist.

"Thank you, Uncle Bakvaasnath," Younguncle said. "This makes my job so much easier."

He leapt down lightly from his tree and inspected the recumbent form of Gobarmal. The man lay unconscious, his thin, cruel lips drawn back in a snarl of surprise.

"Pretty fellow you are," Younguncle said. That gave him an idea.

He went to the pit and looked over the edge. Babu lay at the bottom, also unconscious. Younguncle grabbed one end of the rope and, with some difficulty, managed to haul Babu out and across to where Gobarmal lay. He then lit a small wood fire inside a ring of stones. He rubbed the gray wood ash on the faces of the two men. Then he looked in his pockets and was delighted to find that he still had some of his bangle-seller's wares. He put several bangles on each man's wrist, took out a stick of lipstick, and applied it liberally to their lips. He stepped back to consider his artwork for a moment, then shook his head and put a bright red spot on each man's nose as well.

"Perfect!" Younguncle sighed. "Really, I should go into the beauty business."

He untied the donkey, who had been watching the proceedings with intelligent interest, and managed to strap the two men on to its back.

"This is for a good cause, my friend," he said, giving the donkey a gentle push. "Now off you go—all the way home through the main village to the mansion."

The donkey lumbered away down the dirt track and was lost to sight. Now Younguncle loosed Gobarmal's horse and sent it on its way, too. Then he looked up at the great pipal tree.

"Will you live here now, Uncle Bakvaasnath, and protect the forest from Gobarmal and his kind?"

There was only the wind whispering through the trees. Suddenly a gentle shower of leaves came down around Younguncle. He felt a strange peace pervade his soul.

"I will take my leave then, Uncle."

He loosened Hira's tether and walked with him to the thicket at the beginning of the dirt track, where Bira waited patiently. The two friends greeted each other with small snuffles of delight.

"Now, my friends, I will set you free. Go home to Ancient Uncle! You are both swift as the wind, and no hand can stop you when you are free. Go!"

And off they went.

Only a couple of farmers, bending down in the yellow fields, saw the two animals flash by. They scratched their heads and wondered if they had imagined them. "A god going by on his steed," said one. "That must have been Nandi, Shiva's great bull," said the other. "But whose horse was that?"

Meanwhile, Younguncle bided his time. He meandered through the fields, made a light lunch of bel fruit with a friendly farmer, had a snooze in the deep shade of a jamun tree, and went back into the village of Neelamgiri a little while before sunset.

In the village, people coming in from the fields were gathering in little groups, scratching their heads in wonder.

"I saw it with my own eyes," someone was saying in awestruck tones. "Who could have humiliated the great Gobarmal and gotten away with it?"

"Who is greater than Gobarmal?"

One old man shook his head.

"The gods are showing us what we have always known deep in our hearts—that Gobarmal is nothing but a man. All these years we have thought he, and his father before him, were demons, not men. But if someone can paint his face with lipstick and smear him with ash and parade him on a donkey. . . ."

There was a ripple of laughter, quickly hushed.

Younguncle smiled to himself and went on to the mansion. It glowed in the sunset like a ripe pimple. As he got closer he could hear sounds of commotion from the house: shouts and the high voices of women, and the pattering of many feet.

As he approached the clump of jacaranda trees behind the house, he heard the clatter of steel pots and pans, and the rhythmic squeak of the hand-pump. He let out a sigh of relief. Ranu saw him and started.

"Oh, it's you!"

"I have a little knife," Younguncle said. "I will cut the rope, although your anklet will have to remain for the time being."

She looked nervously toward the house.

"Something has happened. They won't tell me what—I've been here most of the day, doing the washing. The servants even forgot to get me my lunch!"

"Don't worry, we'll find something to eat as soon as you are free."

Younguncle bent to his work. Ranu sprang up when she was freed.

"Will you take me to my maternal uncle's house, brother? He lives in the nearest town. He is poor and humble, and they've probably forgotten that he exists. Nobody will look for me there."

"Yes, we can do that," Younguncle said, wav-

144

ing off her protestations of gratitude. "But before that, I want to make things a little more uncomfortable for Gobarmal."

He had been busily working on the end of the rope that he had cut from Ranu's leg.

"What are you doing? We must run before the servants come to fetch me!"

"I think they may be busy with other things just now," Younguncle said.

He grabbed the frayed end of the rope and flung it into the well.

"Now let's go," he said.

Ranu giggled suddenly. "They'll think I jumped in! All the water supply for the house comes from that well! They'll be afraid to drink from it now."

Younguncle and Ranu made their way through the mango groves and the empty fields. It was almost dark.

"We will go to the main road and try to catch the bus to town," Younguncle said.

It was a long way to the main road, but they helped themselves to mangoes and ber fruit on the way. Younguncle told Ranu the whole story of Gobarmal and Babu and the tiger, and she laughed until she cried.

Finally they came up through the fields to the gray ribbon of the main road. There were no streetlights here, and only a few distant lights pricked through the darkness. They began to walk along the road, eating their mangoes.

Just then a great rumble shattered the night, and twin headlights pierced the darkness. Younguncle leapt into the middle of the road as the bus approached, waving and calling with all his might. The bus came closer and closer.

"Get out of the way!" screamed Ranu.

Among the bus passengers was the man who wanted Younguncle to marry his niece. There were also some other familiar faces. They spotted Younguncle in the headlights, standing in the middle of the road and all yelled, "Stop! It's the young fellow from the human race!"

Ram Lakhan slammed on the brakes, and the bus ground to a halt. Younguncle motioned to Ranu, who came up from the side of the road clutching her mangoes. But before they could climb onto the bus, Ram Lakhan had risen from his seat and almost fallen down the stairs in his hurry. He stood staring at Ranu.

"You!" he breathed. "You're the one I saw in the fair! My beloved! My life's desire! You gave me a mango! Tell me you will be mine!"

Ranu drew herself up to her full height.

"I remember you," she said. "Do you think

I am fool enough to marry any idiot who looks at me with sheep's eyes?"

Ram Lakhan stared at her, ecstasy on his thin, tragic face.

"Goddess!" he said, and fainted.

Ranu looked at him scornfully. She tossed her mangoes to Younguncle. While the entire busload watched, she fanned Ram Lakhan with the end of her sari until he had come around.

"Get me to my uncle's house first," she snapped. "And you'd better drive carefully."

But she was smiling.

It was quite late when Younguncle finally reached home. Ancient Uncle and Ancient Auntie started up as their cook, Bandhu, came bursting in.

"Younguncle's back! Younguncle's back!" he shouted. Ancient Uncle and Ancient Auntie rushed out into the courtyard, and they and

Bira and Hira surrounded Younguncle to give him a hero's welcome.

After he had been fussed over and fed, and had told his story at least three times, Ancient Auntie sent him off to bed. Younguncle lay on the rooftop terrace, watching the great wheeling of stars above his head. The banyan tree no longer rustled when the wind died.

"We will miss you, Uncle Bakvaasnath," Younguncle said sleepily.

The rest of Younguncle's visit passed quite peacefully, if you don't count the affair of the treacherous moneylender, or the great jackal chase, or how Ancient Uncle and Hira came to win a race with a motorcycle, or how Ram Lakhan won (with Younguncle's assistance) the local poetry contest and (without Younguncle's assistance) the heart of Ranu. After two months, Younguncle took his leave and

went home loaded with mangoes, some of which he distributed to the passengers on the bus. The bus was now being driven by a gloomy old man who drove at a snail's pace, lecturing everyone on the futility of corporeal existence.

Sarita and Ravi and the baby were overjoyed to see Younguncle. The whole family had to hear the story of the village visit several times over, while they ate the delicious mangoes. The baby was very proud of the hair from the

tiger's tail and learned how to growl so fero-
ciously that people would say, "Why, Younguncle, you brought home a tiger cub!"

When Younguncle had been back in town for
several months, he got a phone call from his
friend Yusuf with a full report on the status of
the Neelamgiri Sanctuary.

"The new park ranger is doing very well,"
Yusuf told him. "Nobody hunts in the forest
anymore. Thanks for telling me what to say to
the ghost to make it stop throwing branches
down—the ranger is very grateful. In fact, he
goes and chats to the ghost quite often, although
he gets no reply but a shower of leaves.

"The tiger is doing quite well, too. He's too
old to hunt properly, so the ranger started leaving raw meat out for him. Once, the ranger
left the forest rest house to check on something. He had just finished cooking himself a

huge meal, and had left it on the stove to keep warm. Well, when he went back inside he found the kitchen in chaos—pots and pans everywhere and all the food gone. Even the spinach paneer, if you can imagine that! And the tiger was lying on his bed, fast asleep.

"After that the ranger has become the tiger's cook. He keeps sending me letters asking for more and more recipes, especially for paneer. The tiger is quite a discriminating eater, apparently. Amazing, isn't it?"

"Amazing," Younguncle agreed. He smiled at the baby, who was sitting on his lap, thoughtfully chewing the corner of Yusuf's animal book. "But all this talk of food is making me hungry. Why don't you come for lunch? The cook is making spinach paneer and the children are anxious to see you."

"I will come!" Yusuf said. "Perhaps the baby

will teach me how to make tiger noises?"

The baby spat out a corner of page, and eyed Younguncle's shirt with interest.

"*Grrowl!*" she said.

THE END . . .
for now

Acknowledgments

I am grateful to my vast and wonderful family—
parents, siblings, husband, daughter, in-laws,
aunts, uncles, cousins, nieces, and nephews—
for their love, support, and encouragement
through the years.

I'd particularly like to thank my uncle Rajiva
for his support of all my writing endeavors,
and my parents, Leela and Priyaranjan, my husband, Christopher, my daughter, Joya, my sister,
Ruchika, my brother, Ashok, my sister-in-law
Ramaa, and Uncle Vasu for encouraging me by

laughing hysterically while reading the manuscript.

I am eternally in debt to my dog, Jasper, now gone to happier lands, for faithfully keeping me company during the long hours of writing this book.

Many, many thanks also to three friends who field-tested some of the stories on their respective (and unsuspecting) children: Andrea Gauland, Michele Gutlove, and Kurt Kremer.

I am fervently grateful to my unforgettable high school English teacher, Mrs. Devadawson, for her faith in my worth, and to my excellent editor at Zubaan, Anita Roy, for all her help.

Vandana Singh